# All Right Already!

## A Snowy Story

# By Jory John
# Illustrated by Benji Davies

HarperCollins *Children's Books*

First published by HarperCollins Children's Books, a division of HarperCollins Publishers, USA, in 2018
First published in hardback in Great Britain by HarperCollins Children's Books in 2019

10 9 8 7 6 5 4 3 2 1

ISBN: 978-0-00-833003-3

HarperCollins Children's Books is a division of HarperCollins Publishers Ltd.

Text copyright © Jory John 2018
Illustrations copyright © Benji Davies 2018

Typography by Jeanne L. Hogle

Visit our website at www.harpercollins.co.uk

Printed and bound in China

"Ah, another magnificent day.
I love my morning routine."

"Wait a minute. Everything looks. . ."

"...different.

Goodness gracious, it *snowed*! And not just a little.
It snowed a *lot*."

"I've got to tell Bear! He won't believe it.
But it's true, so he'll *have* to believe it."

"Bear! Open up! It's Duck! From next door!
It snowed, ol' buddy! Come on outside and
have a look."

"Grrr. What is it, Duck?
I'm in the middle of my bath."

"Look around, Bear!
There's snow everywhere.
Let's go exploring."

"Not a chance, Duck.
It's *waaaaaay* too cold
out there."

"C'mon, Bear. The snow is so powdery and soft. You can dry off later."

**"Ugh. This seems like a bad idea."**

"What a view! Have you ever seen anything so majestic?"

**"It's too bright. My eyes hurt."**

"Do you want to play freeze tag??"

**"No."**

"Build a fort?"

**"No."**

"Make a snowbear?"

**"No."**

"Come on, Bear. Let's make snow angels together. Then you can go back to sitting around."

"Sigh.

**All right already, Duck.**"

"Okay! Lean back in the snow and move your arms and legs back and forth. Just flap around and. . .

Voilà!"

**"Like this?"**

"Great. Now let's have a snowball fight."

WHAP!

"Isn't this fun?"

**"Not at all."**

"Brr. I'm drenched. I'm going home, Duck. Okay? That's quite enough excitement for one day."

"Whatever you need to do, Bear! I'm just glad we got to experience the magic of winter together."

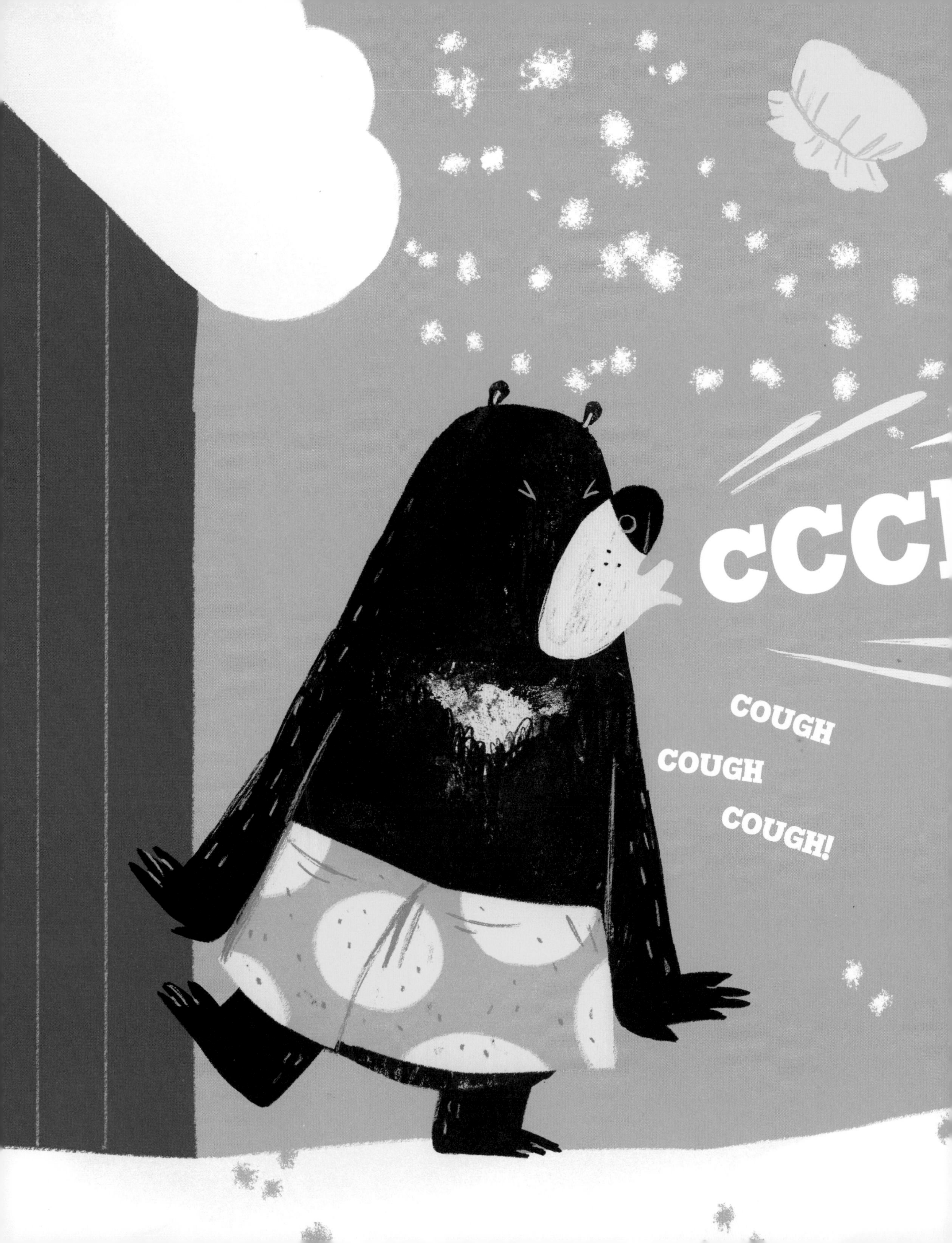
CCC
COUGH
COUGH
COUGH!

# HOOOOOO

RUMBLE
RUMBLE

"Uh-oh."

"Do you want me to wrap you up in blankets?"

**"No."**

"Make you some soup?"

**"No."**

"Put a cold compress on your head?"

**"No."**

"Put a *hot* compress on your head?"

**"No."**

"Make you some toast?"

**"No."**

"Tell you a story from my childhood?"

**"No."**

"Wrap you up in blankets?"

**"You already said that."**

"Please let me do *something*, Bear."

" ALL R

# IGHT ALREADY!

Sigh. How about this: My pillow is flat, Duck.
You can help me with that. Okay?"

"Yes! I'll unflatten your pillow."

**"Okay, Duck. . ."**

"And make you some tea."

**"That's fine. . ."**

"And unflatten your pillow."

**"You already did that."**

"And take your temperature."

**"Ugh."**

"And read you this magazine."

**"No, thanks."**

"And feed you some walnuts."

**"I'm allergic."**

Good Pondkeeping

"Duck, you've GOT to let me rest! That's the only way I'm going to get better. Okay? Right now you're not helping me in any way. In fact, you're just making things worse.

**Out! Now!**"

"All right already, Bear. I'll go home."

"Jeez, Bear's bad attitude is making me feel kind of icky.

COUGH COUGH,

Sniffle.

Maybe I should make some...

AAAAAAH-CHOOOO!

... tea, just in case I'm... starting to get... cough... sick myself.

I don't feel so good. I wonder if Bear will notice and come take care of *me*, just like I did for *him*. That would be nice."

PLEASE TAKE CARE OF ME!

"What on Earth is Duck doing?"

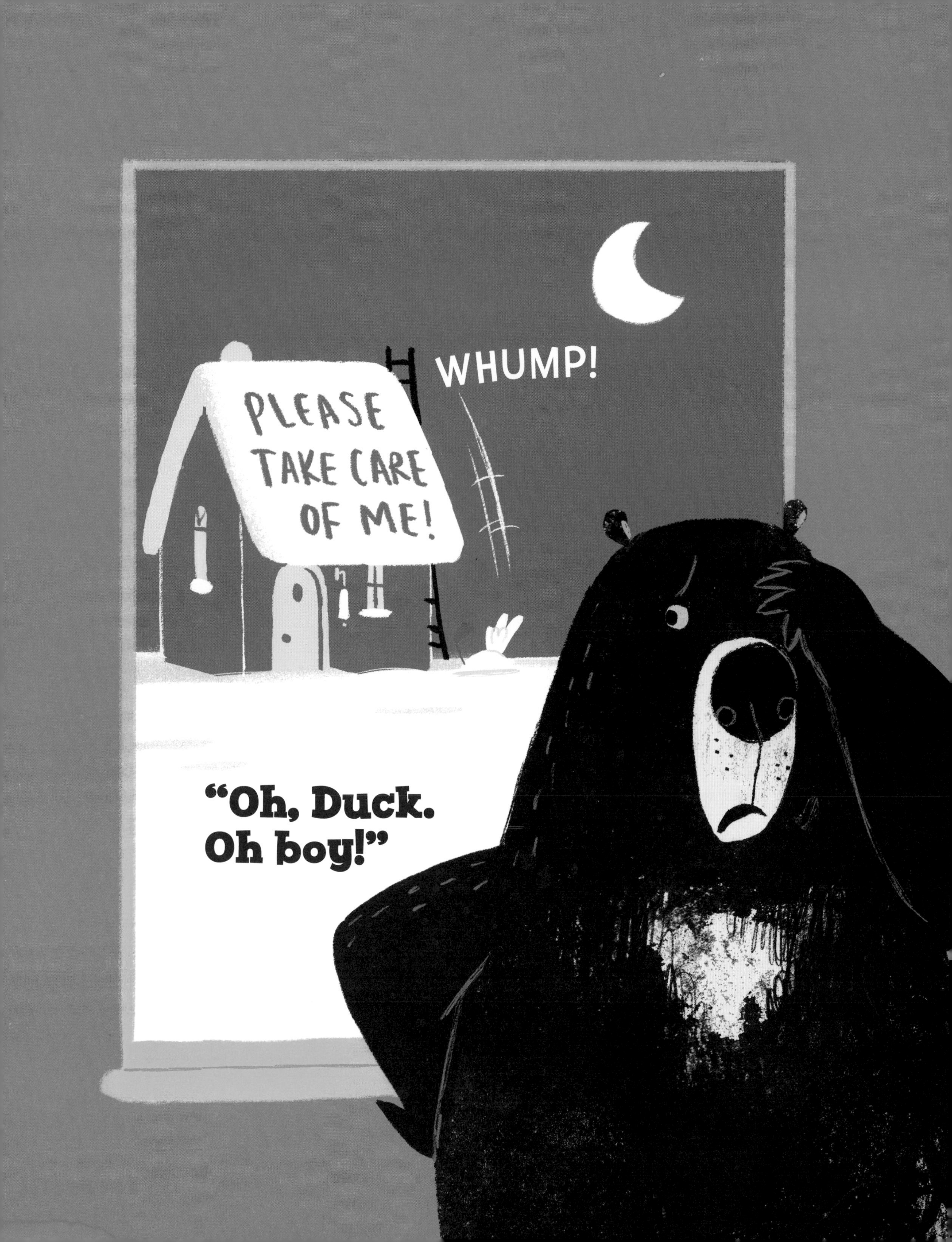


**"Oh, Duck.
Oh boy!"**

"Bear! Oh Bear! You there?"

**"Yes, Duck. I'm in your kitchen."**

"Oh, good. I like my tea really hot, Bear.

And I'm starting to get a little sore.

And my pillow is flat.
Bear? BEAR!

Are you there, BEAR?!"

"GRRR. ALL RIGHT ALREADY, DUCK.

SNIFF

I *must* get some new neighbours."